D0624942

EAST 4TH
MILL STREET
RED CLOUD
JACKSON St
HOWARD
LAKE STREET
SECOND
MAPLE St
RIVER STREET
RAILROAD AVENUE
TERRACE DR
WILLOW STREET
FIRST
WATER
OAK
CHURCH
MADISON
RED CLOUD
SIXTH
HIAWATH WAY
FALLS
HIGHLAND AVENUE
WALNUT
EAST 4TH
PARK AVENUE
JEFFERSON
MAPLE LAKE STREET
MILL STREET
MAIN STREET
VALLEY
HIGHLAND
PARK AVENUE
MAPLE LAKE STREET
4th STREET
MAIN STREET
FIFTH AVE
6th St
JACKSON
WATER STREET
HOWARD
MAPLE AVENUE
MOSINEE
LAKE STREET
FIFTH AVE
SECOND
VINE St
RIVER STREET
RAILROAD AVENUE
CHIPPEWA FALLS WASHINGTON
GRAND AVE
PARK AVENUE
HIAWATH WAY
STATE STREET
THIRD
CHESTNUT
FIRST St
WATER STREET
EAST
MILL STREET
MOSINEE

FOURTH PARK AVENUE
JEFFERSON AVENUE
EAST
MAPLE
LAKE STREET
MILL STREET
MAIN STREET
PARK DRIVE
SEVENTH
COMMONWEALTH
FIFTH AVE
JACKSON St
6th St
1st Ave
CEDAR AVENUE
VALLEY
HOWARD
MOSINEE
LAKE STREET
WASHINGTON
STATE STREET
SECOND
MAPLE St
5th AVENUE
UNION ST
RIVER STREET
MADISON
WATER STREET
FOURTH
CHURCH STREET
OAK
LAKE HICKORY
HUNTER'S POINT
UNION
BIG BULL FALLS
NORTH
HIGHLAND AVENUE
WALNUT
VALLEY
AVENUE
JEFFERSON AVENUE
EAST
MAIN
GRAN
RED CLOUD
MEADOW
HICKORY
BROADWAY
HUNTER'S POINT
MAPLE AVENUE
NORTH
UNION ST
SECOND
RIVER STREET
RAILROAD AVENUE
WASHINGTON
TERRACE DR
FIRST
GRAND AVE
WILLOW STREET
FIRST
WATER STREET
MAIN WOODLAND DRIVE

Выполняя решение Совета [illegible] нашего района [illegible] 8 групп по [illegible] 5—по животноводству. В них [illegible] учебой [illegible] колхозников. В большинстве колхозов эти курсы своевременно приступили к занятиям по утвержденной программе.

Особенно хорошо проходит учеба колхозников в сельхозартелях им. Тельмана (руководители агротехнической группы

Однако не везде еще так развернута массовая учеба колхозников. Например, в колхозе им. Чапаева первые занятия

Особенно хорошо проходит учеба колхозников в сельхозартелях им. Тельмана (руководители агротехнической группы

[illegible] нашего района организовано 8 групп [illegible] и 5—по животноводству. В них охвачено учебой [illegible] колхозников. В большинстве колхозов эти курсы своевременно приступили к занятиям по утвержденной программе.

Особенно хорошо проходит учеба колхозников в сельхозартелях им. Тельмана (руководители агротехнической группы т. Дубровин и зоотехнической группы И. Фаст), им. Карла Маркса (руководитель агротехнической группы Т. Фаст), им. Кирова (руководитель агротехнической группы И. Рамзаев). В этих колхозах проведены по 3—4 занятия. Здесь учеба проводится в тесной связи с производственными делами колхозов. Большое внимание [illegible]

story by
RUSSELL GRIESMER

illustrated by
PRISCILLA WONG

CAPSTONE YOUNG READERS
www.capstoneyoungreaders.com

Every town
is built of stories.

BAKERY
GENERAL
DELI

MAIN
STOP

PUBLIC LIBRARY
CELEBRATING 150 YEARS

Hometown

CELEBRATING 150 YEARS
A TOWN IS BORN
WN HALL OPENS
IS SATURDAY

TEN PAGES
TODAY'S
WEATHER REPORT
WINDY
ALL DRAFTING

The Hometown Gazette
USA MONDAY AFTERNOON
GRAND
THEATER

TO

HARDWARE
GENERAL
STORE

TOWN HALL
DOROT

R&M
MARKET

TOWN HALL
DINER
FORD
REST

URANT
DINER
HOTEL
STORE

TOWN HALL
SCRAP METAL DRIVE
DINER
FORD
RES

GRAND
THEATER
CLOSED

TOWN HALL
RES

KERY
GENERAL
STORE

TOWN HALL
FORD
RES

FRED'S
DINER

TOWN HALL
EQUALITY
LOVE

BAKERY
MUSIC
DINER
T.V.
MAN ON THE MOON

TOWN HALL

RIA
TELEVISION
SALE
SHOE
REPAIR

TOWN HALL
BENEFIT PANCAKE BREAKFAST
REPAIR FUND

HELP
WANTED
SHOE
REPAIR
FOR
SALE

PUBLIC LIBRARY
CELEBRATING 150 YEARS
150th

LOCAL ORGANIC FOOD
150th
NOW LEASING

ELCOME
TOWN

Discover
the stories that built
your hometown.

Many American towns were founded in the 1800s. Shortly after a town was founded, a town hall was often built. The hall served as the town's government center, but the buildings often became the center for important meetings and social gatherings. *Does your community have a place where people gather for work and fun?*

Introduced in 1908, the Model T was the first affordable American car. But that didn't mean everyone bought one right away. Until the 1920s, roads were often shared by cars and horse-drawn buggies. *Imagine if some people still used horses for transportation, while other people used modern cars. What problems could this cause? What would parking lots look like?*

By the 1920s, most small cities had paved streets, streetlights, public electricity, and water systems. This was a huge change from decades past. Work became easier and people had more free time to do things like visit friends and family and go out for entertainment. *Can you think of other inventions that have changed how people live and work?*

During World War II (1939–1945), scrap metal drives were often held to support the war effort. The metal was needed to build tanks, ships, and planes. Children helped gather scrap metal, and often, drives were even held at schools. *What are ways that you and other children in your community help your town or neighborhood?*

Throughout American history, small-town residents have treasured and honored their local members of the military. Parades and ceremonies to mark send-offs, homecomings, and military holidays are often held. *Does your community have any special celebrations to honor the military or other patriotic events? Why are events like these important?*

The 1950s were a time of growth in the United States. Main streets were filled with small businesses of all sorts — everything from shoe shops to ice cream parlors. *Find someone who was a child in the 1950s and ask them to share their memories with you. How is your life different? How is it the same?*

The 1960s was filled with highs and lows. A fight for civil rights for all people led to protests and sometimes violence in communities of all sizes. In contrast, the country came together to mourn the loss of a president and other great leaders and to celebrate landing on the moon. *Space exploration filled the imaginations of many children in the 1960s. Imagine you have the chance to take a rocket into space. Where would you like to go and why?*

In the 1970s and 1980s, some small towns started to see population drops. Long-standing main street businesses started to close, but new businesses sometimes opened in their places. *The illustration shows a group of children hanging out by themselves, playing together. How is this similar to a child's free time today? How might it be different?*

Communities often come together to raise money for special causes, like the town hall renovation in the illustration. *What fund-raisers has your school or community had? Did you help contribute to the fund-raiser in some way?*

IMAGINE & EXPLAIN

Go back and look at the illustrations again, and note how this town has changed over the years. Which time period would you most like to visit and why? Are there any time periods you would not want to visit?

Choose a person on any page. Make up a story about her or his life. What has changed since that person was your age? What has stayed the same?

Choose a building on any page. What happens in that building? Are there buildings like that in your hometown?

What does the word *hometown* mean to you?

Describe your hometown. What do you know about the history of your town?

Imagine you are living in your hometown 100 years ago. What is different? What is the same?

Draw a picture of a building in your hometown. Now draw how you think it looked 100 years ago. Next, draw what you think it will look like 100 years from now.

In this book, the boy is able to see the history of his hometown because of a magical newspaper. At the end of the book, a girl is catching the magical newspaper. What do you think she will learn about her own hometown?

You may not come across a magical newspaper, but there are other ways to learn about the past. What are some that you know about?

FOR MY FAMILY

-RG-

My Hometown is published by Capstone Young Readers,
a Capstone imprint
1710 Roe Crest Drive
North Mankato, Minnesota 56003
www.capstoneyoungreaders.com

Library of Congress Cataloging-in-Publication data is
available on the Library of Congress website.
ISBN: 978-1-62370-174-1 (Hardcover)
ISBN: 978-1-62370-517-6 (eBook PDF)

story and design by: Russell Griesmer
design elements: Shutterstock

Printed in the United States of America in
North Mankato, Minnesota
032015 008823CGF15

FOURTH PARK AVENUE
JEFFERSON AVENUE
EAST
WOODLAND DRIVE
MAPLE
LAKE STREET
MILL STREET
SEVENTH
COMMONWEALTH
MAIN STREET
PARK DRIVE
JOHN F KENNEDY
FIFTH AVE
JACKSON St
CEDAR AVENUE
VALLEY
HOWARD
WASHINGTON
CEDAR FOURTH
MOSINEE
LAKE STREET
STATE STREET
SECOND
MAPLE St
MEADOW
UNION ST
5th AVENUE
RIVER STREET
MADISON
WATER STREET
FOURTH
CHURCH STREET
OAK
LAKE HICKORY
HUNTER'S POINT
BIG BULL FALLS
NORTH
HIGHLAND AVENUE
JEFFERSON AVENUE
EAST
MAIN
MEADOW
HICKORY
BROADWAY
HUNTER'S POINT
MAPLE AVENUE
UNION ST
SECOND
RIVER STREET
RAILROAD AVENUE
WASHINGTON
TERRACE DR
FIRST
GRAND AVE
WILLOW STREET
FIRST
WATER STREET
HICKORY
HUNTER'S POINT
MAIN WOODLAND DRIVE